ElsBeth
AND THE
Pirates's Treasure

ElsBeth
AND THE
Pirate's Treasure

Cape Cod Witch Series
Book I

Written by
J Bean Palmer

Illustrated by
Melanie Therrien

Originally published as
The Cape Cod Witch and the Pirate's Treasure
Library of Congress 2007908286

Holly Hill Press
Post Office Box 662
Farmington, Maine 04938

ISBN 978-1-4951-1881-4

The Story of

ElsBeth Amelia Thistle,

Cape Cod's Youngest Witch,

and her Daring Adventure

with the Notorious Pirate

Billy Bowlegs

TABLE OF CONTENTS

Cape Cod, Massachusetts

Chapter One
Cape Cod, Near the Elbow

Cape Cod, Massachusetts is one of those places in the world that has a history, a long history. Not all of it can be explained.

Right now all seems ideal here. It's another lovely fall day in this postcard-perfect Cape Cod town. Everything is quiet. Nothing unusual is happening. But is some sort of trouble brewing just beneath this calm surface? Is something about to happen?

Let's visit the local schoolroom and see what's up with Cape Cod's youngest witch, her school friends and the local inhabitants. Those who are magical, and those who are not.

Chapter Two
The Little Red Schoolhouse

ElsBeth Amelia Thistle was, at this moment, feeling more than a little upset.

Now that she was in second grade, she was discovering several things not exactly to her liking.

First of all, her teacher Ms. Finch was a mean old thing.

Last year ElsBeth had the cotton-candy-sweet Mrs. Bottomley, and that had worked out just fine. But Ms. Finch was a horror.

This teacher was like something out of those scary movies ElsBeth's grandmother would never let her watch when she stayed over her friends' houses.

And to make matters worse there was this annoying boy Robert Hillman-Jones, who was absolutely driving her crazy.

The worst part of it was that ElsBeth was a witch— granted a small one—but nevertheless a broom-toting, card-carrying, good and true witch.

ElsBeth, though only seven years old, knew several

excellent spells, and if anyone ever deserved to be made into a frog, Robert Hillman-Jones was it.

But she was not allowed to do anything about it. Spells were only to be used for good. And she wasn't supposed to use any magic without supervision.

It was so frustrating.

"Ouch!" squealed ElsBeth, as Hillman-Jones poked her in the ribs for about the tenth time during arithmetic, the one class where Ms. Finch tolerated not the least bit of inattention.

Ms. Finch went to great pains to ensure the students took arithmetic very SERIOUSLY and were ABSOLUTELY SILENT throughout.

At this unheard-of outburst, Ms. Finch turned slowly away from the blackboard, screeching the chalk for what seemed like ages.

The class held their breath as one.

The teacher's beady eyes looked up behind her thick glasses, black, and chained to her head with multi-colored plastic beads.

Ms. Finch was what some people unkindly referred to as "tough on the eyes."

"What was that, Miss Thistle? Did you have something to add to today's lesson in multiplication, perhaps?" Ms. Finch hissed this question sarcastically through tight, thin lips.

All heads turned to ElsBeth.

"No, Ms. Finch," replied ElsBeth.

But before she could stop herself she let slip, "Robert

Hillman-Jones jabbed me in the ribs."

At this forbidden backtalk, Ms. Finch leapt forward at an alarming speed and swept down the row of shocked students, who sat with their mouths open like train-wreck observers. She stopped short at ElsBeth's seat.

"I *heard* that. Apologize at once," she said.

"I will not have children in my class telling tales. *And* trying to get perfectly innocent, dear, young boys into trouble."

ElsBeth pressed her lips firmly together and sat hard on her hands so she didn't say anything that would make Ms. Finch angrier. Or worse, cast a spell in the middle of arithmetic class.

ENTER THE CAT

Fortunately, at just that moment, Sylvanas, her grandmother's unnaturally large, inky-black cat, chose to make an appearance on the windowsill.

The impressive Sylvanas sent a sharp, taunting hiss of his own in Ms. Finch's direction.

The schoolteacher, thoroughly distracted by this newest interruption to the seven's multiplication table, forgot about ElsBeth for the moment.

Ms. Finch stepped cautiously toward the window, nervously flapping her fingers and calling out, "Scat!"

In response to this ridiculous effort to shoo him away, Sylvanas yawned widely. He slowly arched his back, stuck his nose in the air, and plopped rather dramatically onto Amy Clark's desk.

Amy, a small timid girl with pale hair and pale eyes and dressed in pink, was so alarmed she pushed back away from her desk. And her chair abruptly tipped over into Nelson Hamm.

Nelson, a skinny kid with glasses, was at that moment wholly entranced by Amy in all her pinkness, and because of this was completely startled.

He jumped up too quickly and tried to catch Amy, but missed by a long shot, and proceeded to knock his desk into Frankie Sylvester beside him.

Frankie was chunky, but a solid fellow, and was always more than ready to get into a fight. Nelson's clumsiness called for action. Frankie immediately shot up into a classic boxing stance and shoved his puny classmate over.

Unfortunately, Nelson's thin body presented little resistance to his powerful classmate, and Nelson flew in a slow, graceful curve—directly into Veronica Smythe.

Veronica at that particular moment was pleasantly daydreaming about being a teenager with make-up, hip clothes and a boyfriend.

She was *not* happy to be reminded she was still only in second grade, *and* being bumped into by a skinny boy with glasses whose ears stuck out the sides of his head.

Veronica let out a surprisingly loud shriek for a second-grader, at which the rest of the class, until then unaffected, jumped up and began to run around in circles in the general belief that a mouse must have gotten loose in the classroom.

This idea was transmitted by Veronica's piercing shriek, and Carmen Alverez's cry, "Aaah! It's a mouse!"

Carmen, being deathly afraid of the little grey creatures, was always on the alert, and naturally assumed when

Veronica panicked that she must have seen one.

The rest of the class quickly separated into three groups.

Most of the boys wanted to catch the mouse and turn it into a class project.

There was a group of the more squeamish girls, led by Carmen, who leapt onto their desks to avoid the nasty rodent, while their squeals rose up and bounced off the walls.

The third group, consisting of several of the most serious students in the class, including ElsBeth, Lisa Lee and Johnny Twofeathers, followed the action, and the fact that there were no mice in view, with alert interest as events unfolded.

THE CAT IS SATISFIED

The mischievous cat was apparently satisfied that he had caused enough excitement for the moment in ElsBeth's boring arithmetic class.

He propelled himself back to the windowsill and looked over the class with a pleased expression on his flat cat features.

He then licked his lips, gave ElsBeth a slight nod, and took off to find some other dull spot in town that needed his special touch to liven things up.

ElsBeth vowed then and there that Sylvanas would be getting a large bowl of the richest cream she could find for dinner tonight.

She owed him one for rescuing her from Ms. Finch's unnerving attentions.

THE FINCH

Ms. Finch's iron control had been temporarily lost with this chaotic behavior in her normally perfectly obedient and disciplined classroom.

The teacher was somewhat dazed by it all, but gradually began to recover.

She started to get the students back in line. Then the slightly confused look on her face turned into a glare, as her sharp little eyes fell on ElsBeth. The girl was smiling.

As for ElsBeth, she was only thinking about how wonderful Sylvanas could be.

But Ms. Finch once more swept down ElsBeth's row.

The students sensed the sudden change and fell silent under Ms. Finch's completely scary scowl.

All eyes again turned to ElsBeth.

Ms. Finch spat out, "I recognized that cat. You brought him to school and called him in here. Admit it, young lady."

ElsBeth wasn't sure how Ms. Finch knew Sylvanas was a member of her family, but she managed to blurt out, "He's ours, but I didn't bring him to school."

Ms. Finch ignored ElsBeth's answer. "Don't lie to me, girl. You will write, 'I promise not to lie, tattle or disturb the class' on the blackboard three hundred times."

"Neatly!" she added, with emphasis.

With this announcement of punishment, Ms. Finch seemed done with ElsBeth, for now, and strode back to the blackboard. She chalked in:

$$7 \times 6 = 42$$
$$7 \times 7 = 49$$

She whacked the blackboard with the wooden pointer while pronouncing each equation crisply. Ms. Finch was back in control.

WHAT TO DO

Later that afternoon ElsBeth walked home with drooping shoulders, her eyes rarely leaving the sidewalk. She wasn't sure how she could stand school anymore.

Then she got a great idea. Maybe her grandmother could take her out of school and homeschool her. She'd heard the Nye twins were being homeschooled.

Not everyone had to put up with Ms. Finch! Yes, that was the answer.

Chapter Three
The Garden at Six Druid Lane

ElsBeth's Home

ElsBeth began to cheer up with the idea of this much more pleasant future.

She turned down Druid Lane toward the rambling, old Victorian house that was home. And by the time she arrived at the front yard, she was smiling again and skipping along as she often did.

ElsBeth was most usually a cheerful witch.

She soon found her grandmother out back in the herb garden.

ElsBeth's grandmother was a well-respected Cape Cod witch. Nevertheless, Hannah Goodspell did not look to be a grand figure in her gardening clothes.

Plump, with fluffy grey hair pulled up into a bun and delicate wire-rimmed glasses, most people assumed the older witch was just another helpless, dear, sweet old lady. Hah!

Hannah in the Garden

ElsBeth, however, was well aware that Hannah Prudence Goodspell was not a witch to be messed with.

ElsBeth was not afraid of her grandmother. Truly, she loved her to pieces. But she did want her grandmother to always be proud of her.

The young witch hadn't quite figured out how to explain today's events at school in exactly the best light—so that Grandmother would have the whole picture without ElsBeth looking bad, or worse still, childish.

ElsBeth did not wish to be viewed as childish. She knew she had important things she had to learn and to do in life—if she could just figure out what those things were.

Her grandmother quickly solved the problem. "Sylvanas says you got into a bit of bother at school today."

ElsBeth could not see her grandmother's face, as she was bent over the troublesome catnip patch at that moment.

"He said something about arithmetic, and things being at 'sixes and sevens.'" Grandmother's ample figure began to shake. "How I love a good play on words!

"Oh, dear, I should explain. 'At sixes and sevens' is an expression from the old country, meaning that things are jumbled up and confused. Sylvanas told me all about it.

"Also, was there something about blind mice? Or was it 'blind' students seeing mice?"

Hannah's giggles could not be contained and she fell over flat—right into the cabbages.

"Oh, my!" She popped back up, the cabbages no

worse for wear.

"Well, ElsBeth, my dear, what do you have to say for yourself?" her grandmother asked.

"I don't know who is worse, that annoying Robert Hillman-Jones or that toad Ms. Finch."

ElsBeth couldn't hold her feelings in any longer. She kicked the ground as if it were one of her two enemies.

Then she began to smile again when she spied an enormous bullfrog.

He leapt up, landed on the garden stool, and uttered a disapproving "harumph."

"Please don't insult the honor of my close relatives," he croaked in his deep, froggy voice. "Toads may be a little slow, and sometimes lack a developed sense of humor. But I'm quite sure, in all my years, I've never known one to be cruel."

"Well, that's true enough," said ElsBeth. "But I did still want to turn Ms. Finch into a toad."

Both her grandmother and Bartholomew the frog looked at her disapprovingly.

ElsBeth knew that many centuries ago Bartholomew had been a handsome Native American prince named "He Who Beats Bears" (which is its own story for another time). But he had made a powerful witch of his tribe terribly angry when he rejected her attentions.

Bartholomew Before He Was a Frog

The witch had cast a spell on him, and thus his greenness. He'd been a frog ever since.

So this subject was not a laughing matter. ElsBeth had been quite insensitive to mention turning people into amphibians.

ElsBeth hung her head in shame. She had been carried away by her anger at school and had completely forgotten her manners.

"I'm so sorry, Bartholomew." Tears suddenly appeared when she realized what she had done.

Bartholomew said, "It's OK, little one. Actually, being a frog has its moments.

"I used to be extremely good looking as an Indian prince, but I was unbearably proud and empty-headed.

"A couple of centuries as a bullfrog have given me time to look at things differently.

"True, the first hundred years or so weren't so good. I was pretty upset and obsessed with thoughts of revenge. But the last century has been quite interesting.

"And my friendship with Hannah has been truly special."

At that, he smiled and hopped closer. Hannah bent down for a kiss. And for just a split second, ElsBeth saw the most handsome, tall, dark Native American brave where the bullfrog had been.

She blinked, and there was the familiar, old, green Bartholomew sitting comfortably on the garden stool. ElsBeth shook her head.

HANNAH PRUDENCE GOODSPELL

Over the years Hannah and the bullfrog had indeed become dear friends.

The witch taught Bartholomew magical charms most mornings. And Bartholomew taught her the traditional uses of native plants in the afternoons.

That subject contained some of the most important and necessary knowledge for a witch engaged in caring for her community.

The Goodspell witches had only come to the New World in the late 1600's. They had been well schooled for many centuries in the medicinal and magical uses of all European plants. But the New World was different, and this knowledge had to be gained bit by bit.

It was certainly helpful to have the friendship of a

former Native American prince, whose tribal wisdom dated back thousands of years, to gain an understanding of the local plant life and all its important uses.

Sylvanas, who had been missing during the earlier conversations, interrupted Hannah's thoughts of Bartholomew.

The huge cat made a typically grand entrance, appearing out of thin air and landing solidly (as he was a little overweight) right beside Bartholomew on the garden stool.

Hannah Goodspell looked into the cat's brilliant green eyes and knew he was up to something once again.

Sylvanas the Cat and Bartholomew the Frog

"What is it, sir? You look like the cat that ate the cream."

Despite the trouble he frequently caused, Sylvanas never failed to be interesting. Not only did he have an incredible imagination and a pure love of excitement, he always had the latest news. Sylvanas was a terrible gossip and busybody.

He purred. "Yes. I've got a surprise lined up for that prune-faced teacher."

Sylvanas smiled, which in his case meant one corner of his lips turned up a bit. It was a little scary. "I do believe the boys in the class will be unusually pleased tomorrow."

Ignoring all questions from ElsBeth, Bartholomew and Hannah, the cat would say no more about his plans.

He struck a pose, looking like a statue of the Egyptian sphinx, remaining silent and completely mysterious. (He loved being theatrical like this.)

Grandmother ended the pleading from ElsBeth and Bartholomew saying, "It is no use. He's made up his mind. Let's go in.

"I have an apple pie in the oven, which should be done now."

ElsBeth realized she was hungry.

"We have some tasty Cape Cod witch's stew to start. And to go with the apple pie, I made some beach plum ice cream for dessert."

ElsBeth realized she was starving.

They headed inside, except the frog, who could not eat that kind of food anymore— much to his regret.

Chapter Four
A Typical Evening for the Witches

ElsBeth loved her grandmother's witch's stew, a mixture of fresh tomatoes and other vegetables and herbs from the garden, smothered in three-cheese sauce.

It was always served with Anadama bread right out of the oven.

(For those of you who have never had Anadama bread fresh from the oven, you are missing a favorite New England treat made with cornmeal and molasses, and one that smells *most* wonderful while baking.)

With a full belly after the last course of hot apple pie and homemade ice cream—a special delight for Sylvanas—ElsBeth got to her most important studies.

Being a witch involved responsibilities and required daily study and practice. And a lot of patience.

For the last several weeks she had been working on a protective spell for a small kitchen garden.

This was a basic skill for any witch worthy of the name.

She had been practicing on yard-long squares of their garden that Grandmother had marked off with string. She was now on her fifth square.

ElsBeth would have to admit that the plants in first two squares were looking brown at the edges and wilty. She could hear faint, weepy sounds coming from those sections.

The plants there were sadly embarrassed about their poor appearance.

However, each of the last three squares looked progressively greener and plumper.

And now there was a perfect tomato growing fast in front of her eyes.

"Eureka!" she squealed in delight. "I've got the hang of it!"

Her grandmother popped out the back door to see what the noise was about.

She folded her arms and beamed at her granddaughter. ElsBeth was a little impatient, and had a bit too much of a temper, but she was doing all right.

Hannah decided that the littlest witch on Cape Cod was coming along just fine.

Sylvanas and the Garden Shed

Chapter Five
Dreams of Pirates and Treasure

That night in her small captain's bed (with the roomy, built-in drawers underneath where she kept her most favorite things), ElsBeth had dreams. She rarely had dreams, but tonight her dreams seemed almost realer than real.

There was a pirate. He was short and had bowed legs. And there was a cave and gold and jewels and swords, and some men sneaking around.

And there was Robert Hillman-Jones, tied up in muddy rope, looking scared and very cold.

What was Robert Hillman-Jones doing in her dream? It was bad enough she had to put up with him during the day.

"Oh, well," she sighed, still asleep, and she went back into a deeper slumber until the bright morning sun woke her up.

At breakfast her grandmother gave ElsBeth a long, serious look.

"ElsBeth, did you have a dream last night?"

ElsBeth was surprised by the question. "Yes, I did, Grandmother."

"Was it about pirates?" Hannah asked.

"Why, yes, it was!" ElsBeth was shocked by this question. How did Grandmother know?

"We haven't talked about this yet. But tonight, instead of your usual lessons, we will cover a new topic.

"Witch's dreams often have special meanings.

"But enough for now. You'll be late for school if you don't get out the door, young lady."

ElsBeth looked to the tall, moon-faced grandfather clock in the hall—who promptly winked at her and clanged his bells.

She grabbed her half-eaten cranberry-pumpkin-nut muffin and her pack, and dashed out the door.

Calling, "See you tonight, Grandmother. I love you," ElsBeth was off.

Chapter Six
Not Just Another Day of School

ElsBeth and her friends watched the boys in the schoolyard.

The boys seemed particularly obnoxious and secretive today, whispering in a huddled group by the climbing structure.

The girls wondered aloud what they were up to, but the start-of-school bell cut their wonderings short.

Ms. Finch's class settled quickly in their seats. The-one-who-must-be-paid-attention-to did not put up with tardiness or fooling around. That was for sure.

Ms. Finch cleared her throat in a way that sounded like she was going to say something important. "Well, children, instead of spelling, this morning we are going to take up history.

"We will be preparing a special Halloween pageant this year, and the School Board in its infinite wisdom has decided that the time spent can count toward your history lessons."

Ms. Finch spat out this last part as if she didn't think too much of the School Board, Halloween *or* taking credits for a pageant as part of history class.

"Now, you children probably know nothing about the history of Halloween," Ms. Finch said in her I-am-so-much-older-and-smarter-than-you voice.

"So I am going to give you an assignment to ask your parents. Or, in the case of two of our students who don't seem to have any parents," (and at this she looked pointedly at ElsBeth and Johnny Twofeathers) "you must ask your grandparents.

"You are to have them explain to you all about the celebration of Halloween.

"Then you are to write a short essay on the subject, with NO spelling errors and NEAT penmanship. And there are to be no marks outside the lines, or you will have to write your essay over and over again until you get it right.

"Am I *completely* understood?

"Any questions?" She paused a fraction of a second (to ensure no one had time to raise a hand) and went on.

"Now, as to the pageant itself, we have costumes from the previous years in the closet.

"There should be enough for each child.

"One of you boys ... " Ms. Finch's eagle gaze surveyed the room and landed on poor Nelson. "Nelson Hamm ... "

Nelson looked up nervously from his dreamy thoughts of Amy Clark's blond curls.

"Go get the costumes and pass them out," commanded Ms. Finch.

If anyone at that moment had happened to look at the windowsill, they would have noticed a green-eyed, black cat with a sly smile, who appeared to be watching and eagerly awaiting … something.

Nelson's ears turned bright red as he slowly rose from his small desk and shuffled to the classroom storage closet.

The door stuck, and Nelson had to yank hard. Suddenly the door swung wide and hundreds and hundreds of noisy, little grey-brown mice began pouring out into the classroom, squeaking excitedly at the top of their little lungs.

Carmen Alverez broke into uncontrolled screaming. "Mice!! Mice!!"

The black cat's sly smile widened.

The frantic girl started to run in small fast circles around her desk, while at the same time trying to jump up on it.

And on Carmen's signal all the students, even the toughest boys, began hopping up onto their desks and jumping up and down, screaming.

Comfortable on the windowsill, a wonderful observation point, Sylvanas looked on with deep satisfaction at his lovely creation—the unfolding chaos.

ElsBeth was at first amused. But quickly began to worry that some poor mouse would be stomped on with all the jumping around being done.

As the only witch present, she felt responsible for the little creatures.

Ms. Finch had hopped up on her desk, too, and stared down at the mice.

Then her eyes swept across the room, and like a laser aimed straight at ElsBeth.

"ElsBeth, I *know* you have somehow managed to get those mice in here.

"You are in Big Trouble, young lady. Get them out.

"NOW!" she shouted.

ElsBeth decided this was not the time to protest her innocence. She needed to get these creatures safely outside. *And* she couldn't use a spell.

But she could easily speak to them in their own squeaky language, having had many conversations with the little brown fluff balls during her seven years.

So, quietly squeaking instructions, she led the excited little ones out the classroom door, through the wide hallway and down the front steps, as quickly as could be.

The school's principal, Dr. Titcomb, poked his head out his office door just as the floating carpet of mice headed out the front.

He shook his handsome silver hair and blinked several times, but by then they were gone.

He looked down the hall toward Ms. Finch's door then stepped back toward his desk, thumbs in his suspenders, thoughtfully muttering something about, "Have to slow down at happy hour over at the Dan'l Webster Inn."

On the way outside, ElsBeth heard several mice chatter excitedly about Sylvanas. She wondered why they were talking about him.

She looked around for her feline friend, but Sylvanas was long gone—no doubt bored with school now that the excitement was over.

When she returned, the classroom had begun to settle down. The students were seated once again. Ms. Finch had regained the floor and was pacing the aisles.

But the class looked uneasy. You never knew with Ms. Finch.

HALLOWEEN PAGEANT COSTUMES

"Nelson Hamm, I said pass out the costumes," the teacher repeated through clenched teeth.

Poor Nelson, who had been shaking behind the closet door unnoticed by anyone since the mice had flooded forth, jumped into the closet and grabbed an armful of costumes.

He hastily dropped one at each desk as he went around the room.

There was a goblin, an elf, a witch, a pirate, some Indians, a cat, a frog, a turkey, a mouse, a bat, several Pilgrims, a sea captain, a cowboy, a princess and a few costumes no one could figure out, even with extremely creative guesses.

A certain amount of excitement was generated as each student looked over his or her costume, despite Ms. Finch's nasty glare.

The class spent the rest of the morning trying them on and practicing the various scenes Ms. Finch had designed for the pageant.

ElsBeth was pleased that Robert Hillman-Jones was a pirate, just like in her dream.

Well … not precisely like in her dream. In her dream he was a scared little boy. But there *was* a pirate involved. About this she was certain.

There was a lot of grumbling by those who felt their costume was not exactly what they would want to be for Halloween. But most of this was done in whispers. No one wanted to set Ms. Finch off again.

ElsBeth's costume was a bat, which was perfect. ElsBeth's favorite creatures were bats.

People often had funny ideas that bats were scary and sucked your blood and turned you into a vampire.

But that was silly. Bats are actually sweet, intelligent creatures, and the reason they fly close to you in the evening is to take the mosquitoes and other pesky bugs away.

Of course, bats think mosquitoes are delicious, a taste ElsBeth could not quite understand. But as Grandmother often said, "To each his own."

Unknown to her classmates, ElsBeth had a "familiar." A witch's familiar is the one creature, special to that particular witch, who would always help the witch no matter what happened.

And ElsBeth's own familiar was a bat. His name was Professor Badinoff, and he was extremely intelligent.

He was a friendly, but impressive bat, with large, delicately pointed ears. And, in ElsBeth's view, a royal appearance, as if in the bat world he might be a king or a duke or something like that.

Many of the other creatures on Cape Cod thought Badinoff was a brainy snob. But secretly they were proud to have someone so incredibly smart as part of their little community.

Professor Badinoff

On the weekends Professor Badinoff helped ElsBeth with multiplication, a skill that was not coming all that easily to her.

Perhaps this was because Ms. Finch's lessons were boring, stupid and somewhat disturbing with all the loud thwacking of her pointer against the blackboard.

A WITCH'S MARK

Now, not everyone knows that all witches have a witch's mark. It is always in the shape of their familiar— so that no matter what happens, even if they lose their memory, they will always be reminded of the one creature who can help them the most in any situation.

This is not the same type of mark that was referred to in those ridiculous Salem witch stories. Her grandmother had been quick to point this out.

Common moles or a birthmark on quite ordinary girls

were wrongly thought back then to be the mark of a wicked witch. And these unfortunates were the targets of the evil gossips of Salem long ago.

ElsBeth, however, as a real witch of good magic, had the cutest little brown bat mark near the bottom of her left heel.

It was tiny, but if one looked closely it was clearly seen as a bat with outstretched wings.

So, ElsBeth was perfectly happy to be a bat for Halloween.

Veronica, however, took one look at ElsBeth's costume and said, "ElsBeth, yuck! You have to be a bat? Look at me. I'm an Native American princess."

Veronica struck a pose and fluffed her feather headdress dramatically.

ElsBeth's Bat Mark on Her Heel

ElsBeth stuck out her chin defensively. "What's wrong with being a bat?"

Johnny Twofeathers, dressed oddly as a Pilgrim, slid over and pulled ElsBeth away from Veronica.

"Shush! Ms. Finch has it in for you. Don't start anything or you'll be in trouble all week."

ElsBeth just couldn't stand it when people said bad things about bats. She struggled to keep her temper under control.

But good sense finally won out, and she smiled at Johnny and said, "Thanks, Chief."

Johnny was the eldest grandson of a Wampanoag leader, and ElsBeth knew he would be Chief someday. She had known him forever, and since she could talk she often called him that, though no one else did.

Ms. Finch, seeming now to have forgotten the recent distractions, began to arrange her students.

The pageant was to be held the Saturday after next, right before Halloween.

The parents and the whole town would be invited. And following the pageant there was to be a huge Halloween celebration in the auditorium with candy, apple bobbing, a haunted house, a pumpkin carving contest, fortune telling—the works.

The other classes were preparing the decorations, but the second-graders were to be the stars of the show.

The teacher directed the students for their entrance to the stage in each character grouping—the animals, the Pilgrims, the Indians, the mystical creatures. Once this was fairly well learned she had each student group practice stopping in a clever "tableau."

Ms. Finch loved saying the word "tableau," and she explained that the word simply means "a living picture." She had learned the word at her teachers' retreat last summer and used it every chance she could.

Ms. Finch had secret hopes of eventually becoming the drama teacher at Capeside High School when Mortimer Hicks retired someday. (But that is another story, too.)

The teacher then had them practice turning toward the imaginary audience with a little bow, and marching off in a dignified fashion.

That is, Ms. Finch *hoped* the whole pageant would eventually look dignified. "This is going to take a *lot* of hard work," she said over and over to herself. But she gritted her teeth and pressed her thin lips together in firm determination to make it so.

She was set on having an "artistically significant" performance, no matter what.

And after about an hour of serious drilling, the students did actually look at least somewhat orderly, if not completely dramatic.

But with all this rigid classroom behavior, the mischievous nature of Sylvanas, who had stopped by to check on ElsBeth, had once again been awakened.

The cat had quickly become bored—always a dangerous situation with Sylvanas. And he decided that the moment had arrived for him to introduce some more fun.

He felt that ElsBeth and her friends should have an opportunity to make this Halloween rehearsal something to be remembered.

Taking up his perch on the schoolhouse window, he watched Ms. Finch carefully position the students once again, and begin to move them through their serious, slow, no smiling, no smirking, no sound parade.

With a wink of one large, green eye, all the windows along the far wall opened wide, and the ever-ready trickster, North Wind, suddenly and briskly swept through the room.

Hats and masks flew off amid renewed shrieking. Ms. Finch's glasses blew off her head—and then blew right back onto her nose, precisely upside down.

Her short black hair stuck straight up in the air.

And after swirling briefly again through the excited young people, the wind homed in on the helpless teacher.

North Wind twisted around her for several tense minutes, in closer and closer circles.

Ms. Finch tried to escape, hopping here and there. But wherever she went, the whirling wind pursued her.

She began to hop frantically, like a crazy cross between a giant bunny and an African Watusi dancer.

The students stared amazed.

ElsBeth just then happened to look over at the windowsill, and she did a double take. Sylvanas, normally the most standoffish and snobby of creatures, was laughing hysterically.

In his case this most resembled a small panther trying to cough up a giant hairball.

Finally exhausted, Ms. Finch crawled underneath her desk. And the devilish North Wind, unable to maintain a fierce blow in that small space, got tired of the game and left.

As did the cat, greatly satisfied again with his day's "school work" and still chuckling softly to himself.

The rest of the day was comparatively quiet and ended up with things pretty much back to normal by three o'clock.

Finally the bell rang for end-of-school.

All the students hung around outside afterward, as if there were some yet unfinished business.

Veronica stroked her stylish brown locks. Johnny Twofeathers looked like what he was—a young Native American chief, wise and still.

Amy Clark remained a bit fearful. Actually, she pretty much always was. She looked nervously at her toes.

Nelson Hamm looked nervously at Amy Clark. Frankie Sylvester looked for someone with uneaten snacks to share. And Carmen Alverez carefully looked around for any mice that might still be present.

Robert Hillman-Jones burst out the door last, swinging his backpack. "OK, men. It's *showtime!*"

Most of the girls rolled their eyes like, "Oh, my. What do they think they're up to now?"

The boys crowded toward the big apple tree in the corner of the schoolyard.

Frankie Sylvester climbed up as high as he could without breaking any branches. As his mother frequently said, "Frankie is big boned." So he only got about halfway up before dangerous creaking sounds warned him not to go farther.

He was lookout. Someone had to ensure no younger boys, or much worse, the girls, heard the plan or had a chance to get in on the action.

The girls, truth be told, were not at all interested in what the boys were doing, and began to drift off toward home, either by themselves or with a best friend.

Little did they know they would later have reason to regret being so incurious about the boys' plans.

Boys in the Apple Tree

Chapter Seven
Fairy Stories

ElsBeth was especially excited to get home and talk to Grandmother, but she wasn't sure if her grandmother would approve of Sylvanas's pranks. She wondered if it was better not to bring them up.

It would be good if the cat's actions weren't limited in any way. Grandmother sometimes drew the line when Sylvanas got really creative in his fun-loving, trouble-making activities. It would be handy if he had free rein, just in case Ms. Finch got to be too much again.

ElsBeth felt sure the tricky cat could be counted on to create a classroom distraction anytime Ms. Finch started picking on her too badly. She finally decided it would be best not to talk about Sylvanas tonight.

And with the rights and wrongs of what to say (or not say) to Grandmother settled in her mind for now, she took herself down the long, crushed-shell drive, shaded on each side by tall oaks and smaller pine trees.

She soon reached their comfortable old house, trimmed in shades of pink and lavender, and looking over the marsh to the east and then out to the mighty Atlantic Ocean.

"Grandmother, Grandmother, I'm home!" she shouted as she skipped up the front porch steps.

The house smelled so inviting, with hot, spiced cider simmering on the back of the wood cookstove. The scents of cinnamon and nutmeg and cloves and ginger momentarily swept away all thought of the adventures of the day.

ElsBeth helped herself to her favorite drink. She breathed in deeply as she poured it into her very own witch's mug, shaped like a brown bat with his wings touching in back.

She headed back outside with her mug warming her fingers and curled up in the oversized, worn wicker rocking chair on the side porch. She settled in and took a sip as she looked out at the garden.

Grandmother's rather large behind popped up next to a cheery mint plant, from which she was removing some strawberry runners that had strayed from their patch.

ElsBeth knew well that witches had to spend a lot of time in their gardens because plants were so important in their work.

ElsBeth would usually find her grandmother digging away there when she wasn't out and about on other errands, magical and not.

"I'll join you in a minute, dear." Hannah neatly gathered up her gardening tools and said her goodbye to Prince Bartholomew, who had been keeping her company and giving excellent advice on the care of several native herbs.

After cleaning up, Hannah went to the kitchen and poured some of the spicy cider into her own mug. Hers was shaped like a large bullfrog with a curious resemblance to Bartholomew. She joined ElsBeth on the porch.

"Well, young lady, was school any better today?"

ElsBeth considered her reply. "It was very interesting."

Her grandmother looked sideways at ElsBeth's answer, but said nothing. She just smiled wisely and sat in her own, larger green wicker rocking chair.

ElsBeth remembered her school assignment. "We need to write an essay about Halloween and I'm supposed to ask you about it."

Grandmother leaned back, took a sip of her spicy drink, and began to answer slowly in her special teaching voice.

"Halloween. There is so much to say, especially for witches.

"Let's start with some history. It has been celebrated for at least two thousand years. And probably much longer."

ElsBeth had no idea.

" 'Halloween' means 'Holy Evening.' It has always occurred at the end of summer, and many believe it first took place in Ireland and Britain."

Grandmother settled in and began to rock slowly back and forth.

"It is a time when the barriers between the natural and the supernatural worlds are weak or broken. Spirits are close, and are able to pass across into our world.

"Halloween is the most powerfully magical time of the year.

"It might sound odd but in the old days turnips and beets were carved and lit with candles instead of pumpkins.

"These lanterns were, and in some places still are, made to help the ghosts of loved ones who are lost to find their way back to their homes. Or to scare bad ghosts away with a spooky carving if they mean ill."

Grandmother stopped rocking for a moment. She looked up at the clear sky, then into the distance. The creak of the rockers began again as she continued.

"Traditionally, large bonfires are also set to keep the evil spirits away.

"In these times, in most of America, it is just a reason for children to dress up and create mischief and get candy.

"But here on Cape Cod the holiday is still important to many people. Even non-witches here get extra-perceptive, and are apt to see ghosts and goblins, though few would ever admit it.

"To those who are receptive, bits of the future often become clear."

An owl's hoot carried over the marsh. Grandmother paused. Then ElsBeth noticed a small smile appear on her grandmother's face.

"Best of all, the few fairies who made it to America will sometimes let themselves be seen."

"Wow, Grandmother. I've never seen a fairy." ElsBeth straightened up at this startling information.

Hannah looked out to the reds and pinks of the sunset clouds, and she began to cast her mind back.

"It was 1667. I was newly arrived to this continent, having been sent for by your grandfather, a promising, though rebellious, warlock who'd been ordered away to the New World—since he kept causing trouble in the old country.

"Oh, he was a feisty one," she added with a laugh.

"Our ship landed at Boston Harbor safely, despite the rough seas that by all rights should have capsized us not long out of England.

"Fortunately, there were several witches aboard, and between us we were able to cast spells that were effective enough to keep our small craft afloat on the pounding ocean waves.

"When your grandfather met the ship in his small pony cart, he was still anxious for my safety. He had sensed the storms during the crossing.

"You see, we'd been promised to each other for many years—since we could barely form our first spells—and we remained close in spirit, no matter how far the physical distance.

"We were excited to see each other again after all the years of separation. We would finally be able to start our lives together.

"He safely stowed my few belongings that hadn't been lost overboard in the howling storms, and I shyly climbed up beside his handsome figure.

"I had saved one large brocade bag filled with odds and ends given us by relatives—items meant to help us get started in the colony.

"We were on a rough road out of Boston when I heard a strange squeaky noise. It seemed to be coming from the brocade bag.

"I assumed a frightened mouse had somehow gotten trapped inside, and I hurried to let the poor creature out.

"When I opened the bag, however, the squeaking stopped abruptly, and a small scratching noise started up.

"I began to move things around to get at the source of the sounds.

"Aunt Eulaylia had given us a small silver chest as a wedding present, cautioning me not to open it until my wedding day."

Aunt Eulaylia in the Old World

"Well, that very day was to be my wedding. Nathaniel and I were to be married as soon as we got to Salem. The small community of witches there would conduct the ceremony and host our wedding celebration.

"But the scratching got so insistent I forgot all due caution and just opened the jeweled silver box without a thought.

"And what do you suppose was inside?"

"I don't know, Grandmother. What?" ElsBeth could barely breathe.

"The maddest, tiniest pair of fairies that eyes ever set on. That's what.

"Aunt Eulaylia felt sorry for us being in the New World without any fairies to keep us company, so she had enchanted a young fairy couple that her cat, Lord Farthingales, had captured.

"She cast a spell on them so they would sleep through the journey. And with the utmost care had placed them in the silver box, which she'd lined in plush, red velvet so they'd slumber in comfort on the long, dangerous sail across the sea.

"They had now woken from their enchantment and were very displeased with the state of affairs.

"Fairies can have terrible tempers when provoked," she added, shaking her head at the memory.

"I can tell you my heart was in my throat. If we hadn't kept that Pilgrim ship afloat, those two magical beings might have been lost to the world. Or worse, captured by Neptune in his undersea kingdom—and he has more than enough magical horsepower already, thank you very much!

"When I looked closely at them I saw the most perfect, delicate creatures with green and purple wings—like little hummingbirds. But the effect was spoiled when they opened their little rosebud lips.

"The words that came out of those two would make an old sailor blush to his toes. And their voices—they would pierce your ears.

"And they had steely, sharp, little teeth, too.

"Nathaniel and I were so stunned we forgot to clamp down on the lid right away. And with gleeful, high-pitched laughs, and several unseemly taunts, the fairy couple flew close to our noses once, then twice.

"They sneered. Both of their perfect, tiny faces

expressed smug triumph. They had escaped a powerful enchantment after all.

"But before they left, they looked us up and down. I think they found us fools to have let them escape so easily. But despite that, they seemed to accept our magical kinship. After all, witches are first cousins to all fairies, as well as elves and goblins.

"Mostly, I'm sure they were happy to be free of any spell or obligation to us—which would have been the case if we'd been just a hair quicker and snapped the lid down fast.

"The only other time I've ever seen a fairy since leaving the old country," Hannah continued, "was right before the Salem witch trials.

"It was the night of the full moon, which had risen huge and pumpkin-colored in the sky, as it often does on crisp, fall evenings in this part of the world. It wasn't long after dusk and Nathaniel and I were fast asleep on our farm when we were suddenly awakened by an insistent tapping at the window.

"Nathaniel got up and saw a small blur outside. We didn't have windows you could open in those days so he threw on his cape and ran outside to find out what it was.

"He had hardly opened the door when the very same two fairies buzzed his ears. They warned him that we had to leave Salem that night, and told us where we must go.

"Fairies aren't generally very thoughtful creatures. In fact, they are usually tricksters and can't be trusted at all.

"But it seemed they hadn't found much in the way of magic they were used to in the New World, so they'd apparently decided to adopt us to help protect what little familiar magic there was here.

"Nathaniel and I were a significant portion of the local magical community back in those days.

"Nathaniel quickly told them where other witches we knew could be found so they could get to safety, too.

"And the tiny beings were off in a wink, leaving a trail of golden glitter across the cold night sky in their wake.

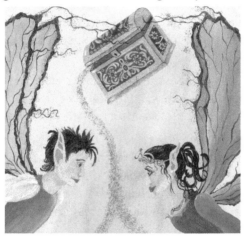

The Fairies from the Old Country

"We packed up our pony cart and awakened Sylvanas, who was deep asleep by the hearth—he's always been an unnaturally sound sleeper.

"We gathered the treasures I'd brought from the old country, and within the half-hour we were heading south for Cape Cod, and away from those dreadful witch trials.

"I've never seen those fairies or any others since that night, at least not directly. But they surely are around. One sees the signs now and then."

Hannah sat back and sipped her cider.

"Well, ElsBeth, you certainly got me going. Halloween is a great tradition and I'm glad to hear your teacher is having you learn of it."

ElsBeth prickled a bit at the idea of praise for her archenemy Ms. Finch. But perhaps Grandmother was right. Ms. Finch surely couldn't be *all* bad.

And the pageant was sure to be fun, as well as the party with all the treats and apple bobbing and pumpkin carvings and the haunted house.

She was busy imagining all these delights when Grandmother brought her back to earth.

"It's time to peel the vegetables and get supper on the table. Come into the kitchen and help, please, ElsBeth."

Even witches have to do chores.

Tonight's dinner was especially delicious with potato leek soup, and cabbages stuffed with tomatoes, herbs and flavorful cheeses.

The crusty bread was straight from the oven, and there was fresh butter from Farmer Green's lovely cow Beatrice.

And for dessert they had cranberry-black walnut tart with whipped cream.

On several occasions Grandmother had told ElsBeth she was lucky to be a witch. "Other children often have to eat 'fast food,' which is not natural at all."

Grandmother always shook her head sadly after she said this.

ElsBeth decided some day she would learn to cook as well as her grandmother. Cooking, she could see, was definitely an important skill for a witch.

It was hard to cast a decent spell on an empty stomach. And witches, and even non-magical people, clearly did best with tasty, nutritious meals in their bellies.

After dinner they settled in by the fireplace. The days were starting to cool off, and there was a chill to the evening.

Grandmother and ElsBeth each sat on the plump cushions of the faded-blue wing chairs and now sipped hot chocolate.

Soon Grandmother began to speak of dreams.

"Part of being a witch is knowing what the future is likely to hold. If you have some warning, you can often influence events for the better, and even sometimes prevent a tragedy.

"No witch can completely control the future, of course. But many who have seen the future have been able to have a strong influence for good ... or ... the opposite," she added.

Grandmother almost whispered these last words. She shivered a little, as if casting off a bad memory. But she continued.

"ElsBeth, dreams often tell us things we wouldn't otherwise know about the future. You may be able to piece together bits of things you observed during the day, or even from weeks before. And understand things you would not otherwise have been able to realize.

"Also, when the body rests, the spirit is sometimes free to roam about in this world. And you can see things you could never see any other way.

"We witches do not often dream, but when we do it is important.

"And I'm worried about the dream you had. There have been other signs that some danger is about near the village.

"And it is almost Halloween, when, as I said, the spirit world and the everyday world are much more closely connected than usual.

"We must pay attention. I fear that something quite disastrous could happen if we are not alert.

"Tonight I'm giving you your own diary.

"If you dream again, the moment you awaken you must write everything down immediately. No matter how silly it may seem at the time, it may help to avoid a terrible tragedy in the future."

With that warning, Hannah handed ElsBeth a purple, leather-bound journal with lined pages and a lavender, velvet ribbon to mark her place. A small, silver bat weighted the end of the ribbon.

The diary felt light, but all these new responsibilities weighted ElsBeth. She felt serious. And she was worried that her grandmother would think her dreams so important. She clutched the diary to her small body.

"I understand. I promise I'll write everything the minute I wake up."

That night, wrapped in a pink, flannel nightgown embroidered with tiny brown bats, the young witch slept deeply. But this night, there were no dreams.

Chapter Eight
Back to School

Excitement built at school over the next week and a half as students, teachers and even parents began to prepare for the Halloween pageant and party.

The ordinary had to be endured, though. Multiplication tables were practiced, spelling lessons were learned.

Reading classes were sweated through, by many. When it came to reading, Ms. Finch was *very* particular about e-nun-ci-a-tion.

Reading aloud with Ms. Finch interrupting at each hesitation, mispronunciation or stumble was a nerve-wracking experience dreaded by most. It was worst for poor Nelson Hamm. He had a slight stutter anyway and never liked to be called on.

ElsBeth, fortunately, was a good reader. Her grandmother had read to her since she was a baby.

Witches, as a rule, Grandmother said, don't watch much television. They didn't even own a television in fact. "There's too much to do in the real world!" she'd often tell ElsBeth. At their house books, puzzles and word games were their main entertainment, once chores and lessons were done, of course.

From age four, ElsBeth had liked to read with her own voice. Pretty much all witches, Grandmother said, loved the sound of their own voices.

Grandmother had been patient as ElsBeth had stumbled her way through the words at first.

She'd never been interrupted or criticized, and now she was a natural and fluent reader.

And as a witch, she had an uncanny ability to imitate animals and people.

If anything, ElsBeth had to restrain herself from being *too* realistic when she read aloud.

Ms. Finch required precision—but emotion and drama were just not allowed.

And so, aside from the occasional painful reading experience for one student or another, which ElsBeth felt was just too bad, the only thing of note that happened while waiting for Halloween to arrive was in the pumpkin-carving class.

They had art class once a week. But instead of the usual finger painting, leaf tracing, or the creation of ceramic palm-print ashtrays, Ms. Finch was allowing this special, pumpkin-carving class.

She wanted especially to monitor this pumpkin carving activity herself. A lot was at stake. A huge lobster trap filled with candy, donated by the Penny Candy Store in Centerville, was the prize for the best carving.

The students soon learned that Ms. Finch was deathly opposed to cheating. There was at least one lecture a day on the subject.

This meant that help from brothers, sisters and parents was strictly forbidden.

Just yesterday Ms. Finch had proclaimed, "All children are natural cheaters." And then added, under her breath, "and worse."

At this, the students had looked around suspiciously at each other.

They hadn't realized they were all cheaters, though for sure Veronica *had* intended to ask her mother, a well-known Cape sculptress, for some help with her carving.

Ms. Finch ordered each child to bring in his or her own pumpkin of no greater than ten inches in diameter, and they would do the tracing and carving under her strict supervision.

On the carving day each student also had to line his or her desk with layers of old newspaper. Pumpkin carving was known by everyone to be extremely messy.

An apron of some sort also had to be brought from home, and there was quite a variety of these to be found amongst the classmates.

Amy had a frilly pink thing just her size. Nelson had a large red one with "Baste Me" in big black letters on the front.

Jimmy, whose father was a local lobster fisherman, had a highly effective old yellow slicker, though it gave off a slightly fishy smell.

Lisa Lee's apron had a faded picture of Albert Einstein covered with complicated mathematical formulas.

Veronica wore something artful, with embroidered

butterflies floating around amidst graceful, green dragonflies—no doubt purchased from one of the trendy Chatham shops.

ElsBeth had on one of her grandmother's aprons, decorated with shimmering green and gold rainforest frogs.

All the students were well armed with identical orange, plastic pumpkin carving tools and black Magic Markers and quickly got to work.

ElsBeth made a charming bat with a lopsided smile and big ears.

Veronica made a sprightly goblin. No doubt her mother wasn't the only talented one in the family.

Jimmy made a lobster, which was a new twist on Halloween, but he pulled it off by making it extremely scary.

Lisa Lee had taken a perfectly symmetrical pumpkin and precisely carved her hero, Albert Einstein, doing an amazing job on his hair.

No one quite knew what Nelson Hamm's carving was. Some thought it was a rat, but two classmates who knew a lot about art agreed it was a Salvador Dali-style werewolf.

Nelson's carving sparked the greatest debate, and at least one fistfight, when Frankie Sylvester defended his interpretation to Jimmy Miller.

Johnny Twofeathers made an osprey—an eagle-like bird well loved on the Cape.

Amy made a kitten.

Several of the carvings done by the class turned out to be minor works of art.

To everyone's surprise, even after all the long, daily lectures on cheating, Robert Hillman-Jones had brought a *Family Circle* magazine pumpkin-carving pattern to trace, and kept sneaking a look at it under his table.

He kept his carved pumpkin carefully hidden under newspaper while he worked. Finally, at the end of class, Robert Hillman-Jones revealed his creation.

It was cut into on an extremely squat, rare, white pumpkin, which *every*one swore was not within the ten-inch limit.

It was an incredibly detailed design with a half-moon, a wart-nosed witch on a broom, a cat with spiky fur, and curlicues of ivy laced around the back and sides.

The students stared open-mouthed with indrawn breaths. They'd all seen him use the tracing paper he tried to hide in his lap.

The room went silent. All together they looked up for Ms. Finch's terrible reaction to his obvious cheating.

Ms. Finch walked slowly over to Hillman-Jones's desk. Robert smiled up meltingly.

Suddenly a brilliant smile broke through on Ms. Finch's normally frowning face, and she actually giggled girlishly.

Two students in the back dared to sneak a look at each other.

"Well, I'm not sure what the other classes have come up with, but this is certainly the most impressive carving I've seen in the long history of Capeside Elementary School.

"Well done, Mr. Hillman-Jones! Well done, I say!"

ElsBeth steamed. How could eagle-eye Finch not know he cheated?

Veronica's pumpkin should have won, no question, if it weren't for Hillman-Jones's dishonesty.

ElsBeth was about to burst forth with a not very well thought out complaint, which surely would have gotten her another long punishment, when she felt Johnny Twofeathers's hand on her arm.

"Don't do it," he whispered. "She just wants him to win.

"If you say anything, he'll still win but you'll be in big trouble.

"It's Halloween. You don't want extra assignments now."

Johnny's wisdom seeped in, slowly, and ElsBeth deflated like an old balloon.

Johnny was right. And brave, too, to risk whispering in Ms. Finch's class. Ms. Finch was death on whispering.

ElsBeth had to let it go.

THE BOYS' PLAN

Later, when the school bell rang, the boys made a beeline for the apple tree.

Whatever scheme they had been working on the last few weeks seemed to be shaping up.

ElsBeth and the other girls looked on and asked themselves what the boys were up to.

Veronica said, "Those boys are planning a major toilet-papering of the town. I just know it!" She shook her head of glossy brown curls.

After further talk it was broadly agreed amongst the

girls, based on no real evidence but definite and strong opinions, that Veronica was right, or possibly the boys would try to climb the church bell tower and leave some silly sign.

It would be mildly courageous and mildly entertaining, but the girls really didn't expect too much.

Silly girls!

Pumpkin Carvings

Chapter Nine
Halloween—The Big Day

And so the days went by. Right up to Halloween, which fell on a Saturday this year, which was wonderful.

The students would have all day to decorate the auditorium, and set up the best haunted house ever.

It would even have small rooms where you could stick your arm through a curtain and feel squishy things. There would be bowls of peeled grapes for eyeballs and cold spaghetti for brains.

It was going to be really gross and spooky, especially with Mr. Sparks's special effects.

Mr. Sparks used to work in Hollywood for the famous movie director Steven Spielberg.

It was rumored around town he'd had a "meltdown," and was back on the Cape recovering far away from that "viper's nest" in Los Angeles, California.

ElsBeth knew a viper was a kind of poisonous snake. But she wasn't sure they lived in nests and she really didn't think they lived in Hollywood. But Mr. Sparks seemed pretty OK to ElsBeth and her friends.

He was a little nervous and jumped at the slightest sound, but he really loved creating scary lighting effects that came on when someone was about to walk by.

Between Mr. Sparks and Veronica's mother, who made the ghosts and witches that popped up when someone passed near, it seemed like this would be the best Halloween celebration ever held in this small Cape Cod town.

Students and parents began drifting in around seven-thirty on the morning of the big day.

Around nine-thirty it became obvious that something was missing. Or more accurately some*ones* were missing. There was not one second-grade boy there.

Nelson Hamm's father was the first to mention it.

"Say, my boy took off early this morning and said he'd meet us here. That was almost three hours ago."

Soon several other parents were saying much the same thing. The boys had all left early and not been seen since.

It was assumed by the adults that some Halloween prank was in the offing, and no one got too worried until lunchtime rolled around with still no sight of them.

None of the boys were known to have taken any food with them, and several were famous for not being able to go more than an hour without whining about being "completely starved" and begging for food.

Finally, at five minutes past noon, Frankie Sylvester's dad, who was also Town Constable, stepped slowly up onto the stage.

He was tall and broad and had a firm jaw. Constable Sylvester was someone everyone in town knew and respected.

He called out calmly in his low policeman's voice, "Now folks, gather round please. It seems like several of our boys from the second-grade class are missing.

"I'm sure it is nothing to worry about. Boys like to pull pranks, especially on Halloween. I know I did when I was that age," he added, and a few people chuckled.

"But they've been gone longer than they should, so we ought to set about finding them. Does anyone have any idea where these kids could have gone?"

The auditorium broke out in nervous whispers, until Veronica Smythe stuck up a small, insistent arm.

"Constable Sylvester, we've noticed the boys planning something for weeks."

The constable thanked her gently and inquired, "Did any of you students overhear anything about what they were planning?"

Carmen Alverez spoke up. "We couldn't. Frankie was lookout and wouldn't let anyone near enough to—" Carmen stopped mid-sentence when she realized it was Frankie's dad she was reporting to.

Constable Sylvester cleared his throat softly and said, "Thank you, Carmen."

No one else had anything to say, so the constable announced, "Well, it looks like we are going to need a search party.

"Those boys could only have gone on bicycles and it's only been a few hours. They can't be far.

"We'll break up into groups, each with a leader.

"You children stay here and continue with the Halloween party preparations. We don't want to have to search for anyone else.

"We'll find them and have them back in no time, all set for the celebration."

He tried to sound cheerful, but everyone could hear the tinge of worry in his voice.

There were hundreds of years of history in the small Cape Cod town, and missing people had happened before.

In fact, there were stories that circulated now and then that every fifty years a group of townspeople went missing and were never found. Or so the legends went.

As the constable rounded up the adults and gave out assignments for search areas, ElsBeth quietly moved toward the back door behind the stage.

Before she got out, several girls in her class surrounded her.

Veronica seemed to be the spokesperson. "ElsBeth, we know you're going to look for them. Take us with you, we can help."

ElsBeth whispered back. "Quiet, you'll get their attention, and none of us will be able to leave."

Right or wrong, ElsBeth thought she could do better alone. But when she looked over the worried but determined faces of her friends, she decided she couldn't leave them.

So, making themselves very quiet and natural looking, one by one Ms. Finch's second-grade class, girls section, made its way behind the maroon velvet stage curtain and slipped out the back.

ElsBeth led them quickly to the nearby woods where they wouldn't be seen.

They already had their Halloween costumes on, but it

was too late to do anything about that.

The girls huddled around ElsBeth and waited for the plan. ElsBeth waited for the plan, too.

"OK, what do we know?" ElsBeth said. "Constable Sylvester already asked, but let's think hard. Did anyone see where the boys have been going after school?"

Small faces tightened in concentration.

Amy, in her pink fairy costume, looked scared. "Well, I saw two of them on their scooters hanging around town in the last week. But this morning I think I saw Jimmy take off on his bike on the road to the old lighthouse."

ElsBeth said, "Very good, Amy. Anyone else?"

Costumed Girls in the Woods

Veronica said, "You know, I saw Robert Hillman-Jones in the Eastern Mountain Sports store in Hyannis last Saturday. He bought three sets of those headband flashlights and several collapsible sacks.

"I just thought he was over-preparing for trick-or-treating—you know Robert. But maybe that's a clue. Why would he buy *three* headlamps?"

"Right!" ElsBeth felt they were getting someplace now. "Good work, Veronica."

Suddenly ElsBeth's dream came back to her. Robert Hillman-Jones in a cold damp cave, and a pirate and his booty.

ElsBeth nearly shouted. But caught herself just in time and whispered instead. "I have an idea. I think they're after Billy Bowlegs's hidden treasure."

The girls gasped. They'd all heard of Billy Bowlegs. Everyone in town had.

Back in the times when this country still belonged to England, Captain Billy was a famous pirate who'd gone after ships carrying Spanish gold.

He was most known for his thievery in and around the Caribbean. But he also had a sweetheart Verity Hope Hoxie right here on Cape Cod.

The stories went that Captain Billy had brought all his gold back to the Cape as a wedding gift for Verity Hope, and that the treasure was still hidden somewhere in a cave here.

Part of the legend went there was a jealous rival for sweet Verity's hand. And when Captain Bowlegs and his men were hiding the gold, Verity Hope's other admirer, Captain Ebenezer Toothacher, had followed them into the secret cave.

And in the fiercely fought sword fight that resulted none had survived, and the treasure and its location were lost forever.

It was said that both ghosts were restless—always searching for Verity Hope. And that Captain Bowlegs still jealously guarded his treasure.

Some said the two didn't even know they were dead. And on rare lonely nights in October they could be heard arguing and clanking swords.

Other folks with more common sense (and less imagination) said it was "the wind blowing through the rigging" or "the waves on the buoys" or "chains holding the boats in the harbor" that made the noises.

But when the chilling sounds came, as they often did on those certain nights, anyone who heard them felt the shivers run up and down their spines.

Veronica was the first to recover. "Everyone knows that's just an old tale."

"Maybe," said ElsBeth. "But you know Robert Hillman-Jones. Do you think that would stop him?"

Veronica thought about that. "No, that would probably only make him more interested."

"Right," said ElsBeth. "They must think the gold is in the caves just beyond the old lighthouse. We need to get there as quickly as we can."

Fortunately, everyone had on sturdy sneakers, as they'd all prepared for maximum-speed trick-or-treating.

"Let's go!" And with that, the small band of girls took off, following the deer path through the woods that would take them toward the lighthouse on the point, and the dark, damp caves beyond.

Chapter Ten

Hannah Goodspell Gets Involved

Back at the purple and pink Victorian house on Druid Lane, Hannah Goodspell listened attentively to Sylvanas, who had witnessed the stir at the auditorium.

The cat had stayed just long enough to get the details, as was his habit. He had then picked up all the bits of news from around the town. He quickly brought the elder witch up to date on what he knew about the missing boys.

He was not, however, aware that ElsBeth and her band of second-grade girls had become involved in a secret rescue attempt of their own.

Hannah shook her head and briskly pulled off her apron. "My, my, so it happens once again."

Hannah had been around during each of the previous disappearances, and despite her magical efforts, she had not been able to find the townspeople who had gone missing.

This time, hearing it was a pack of young boys from ElsBeth's class, she was more determined than ever they should be found safe and sound and returned to their families.

She quickly decided the best strategy was to first get the local animals involved in the search.

They could cover much more territory, and were shy of people so they always had a good idea where people were. Boys, especially young boys, in the animals' habitat, were always noticed.

Hannah ruled out anywhere in the village as a likely hiding place. It would be almost impossible for a handful of them not to be noticed in town, particularly with all the Halloween activity going on today.

Sylvanas would round up the cats, including all the feral cats, the wild ones, who'd be the sharpest lookouts. He would brief them and put them on alert.

Bartholomew, who had been nearby and listening carefully while Sylvanas told his shocking news to Hannah, was quick to offer his help, too.

"I can get the marsh frogs, the field toads and at least some of the fish to help. I hope we get no answer from the fish, though, as it could mean only the worst if the boys have fallen into their domain," he croaked sadly.

An enormous blue heron named Thaddeus Crane, the long-legged (and long thinking) water bird who often visited the marsh behind Hannah's house, said he would call up the help of the seabirds.

He added huffily, "The land birds would be of no assistance, being that they are all mindless creatures only interested in bugs, berries and the latest bird gossip."

Hannah thanked Thaddeus and described the pack of boys so he could pass on the description to the eagles and ospreys, whose sharp eyes would be most needed.

Hannah wanted to call upon the Cape deer and hare,

too, but they were so nervous and easily alarmed she felt she couldn't afford the time it would take to approach them without scaring them off.

She also couldn't ask the bats, as it was now broad daylight and they would be completely blinded by the bright sun and of no use.

With the local animals now assisting in the search, Hannah decided to take her bicycle and visit the Wampanoag medicine man next. He had his own friends among the creatures, and his people may have already heard something.

She quickly tied on a large green hat and a plaid wool cape. The cape looked just like those expensive ones from the Puritan shop, but hers was an original from the old country, woven with magic.

Hannah felt to her toes she would need all the magic—and luck—she could find.

She then cast a simple speed spell on her bicycle, which leapt ahead just as she was jumping on. And with cape and hat flapping wildly, the older witch was off.

Hannah Goes for Help

Chapter Eleven

The Girls Continue the Search

Meanwhile ElsBeth and the girls were halfway to the lighthouse. Some of the girls were beginning to wonder what they had gotten themselves into.

Carmen was not so sure about going into a cave. "ElsBeth, what if it is slimy? What if there are … mice!" she said with increasing alarm.

ElsBeth tried to calm her down. "You can stay outside. We'll need a lookout anyway."

Veronica, on the other hand, was completely confident, even eager. She had begun to daydream about being a hero and having her picture in the paper—maybe even on TV.

She had just bought a new sweater, and she could borrow her mother's gold necklace—the one with the shells set between polished beads of sea glass. With any luck she would look at least ten, almost a teenager.

ElsBeth could only concentrate on Robert Hillman-Jones and the boys. At least they had Johnny Twofeathers with them.

Johnny was smart, and a Native American, which, in her opinion, meant he should have no small ability when it came to dealing with ghosts.

The girls had come to the marsh grass now and decided not to chance the road. The marsh grass was tall enough to easily hide them. After all, none of them were over four feet.

They would have to be careful of the tide. It was pretty low now. And ElsBeth thought they could make it to the lighthouse before the tide rose and the marsh flooded, cutting them off.

That was her thought.

But would they?

Chapter Twelve
Hannah and the Wampanoags

In no time at all Hannah made it to the Legion Hall where Eddie "Wily" Coyote, the Wampanoag tribe's shaman, or medicine man, spent most of his days informally running local tribal affairs.

Inside, the Legion Hall was almost completely dark, and most of the eyes that turned toward her were like bright sparks in the shadows.

But she was able to make out Eddie Coyote's deeply wrinkled face and went over to him.

"It is good to see you, my old friend. Greetings and best wishes," said Hannah. One needed to keep up one's manners, no matter how desperate the situation.

"I have some worrying news, though. It has happened again, my friend. A group from the town has gone missing."

Eddie Coyote looked at Hannah closely. "What business is it of the tribe if foolish tourists get themselves lost and disappear?

"Ignorant outsiders often get themselves misplaced, or

shipwrecked, or killed with drink." Missing tourists wasn't a subject that interested him much.

Hannah quickly explained. "Well, this time it's a group of young boys from the town, and one of them is Johnny Twofeathers, grandson of Lester Killfish and your great, great nephew, I believe."

At this news, Eddie Coyote sat up straight. "Johnny can be a little reckless, but he's not a fool. What is he doing with a pack of lost schoolboys?"

Hannah tried hard to keep the impatience out of her voice. She needed his help.

"I don't know, but we've got to find them before something happens."

Wily Coyote now understood. But instead of leaping into action, he slumped into a deep trance.

He was so completely still not even a hair on his head moved for what seemed like ages. But it was, in reality, only a matter of minutes before he shifted in his chair.

The old man shook himself, pulled his shoulders back and straightened up again.

His face became serious and he told the witch directly, "They are after Billy Bowlegs."

Hannah did not question how he knew. Witches weren't the only ones with powers beyond the ordinary.

With a shiver, she recalled that everyone she'd ever heard of over the centuries who went looking for Billy Bowlegs's pirate treasure had ended up either disappointed, or had disappeared and was assumed to be … gone.

"We need to find them. Now," she almost yelled. Then, quieting herself, she asked, "Will you come?"

"Yes." The medicine man said. "If Johnny Twofeathers is with them, they will get close to the gold and they will need help.

"I'll get Pete Eaglesbeak to take his crop duster airplane up for a look, and we'll get the fishermen with boats to check the shoreline.

"It's too bad—they should leave Billy Bowlegs to his gold. That pirate will never give up his treasure. It has been well over two hundred years and no one has got it yet."

He spat a wad of tobacco into the nearby brass spittoon and got up, ready for action at last.

Hannah knew that Wily and his friends would be in the air and on the water in no time.

She had no idea herself where to start searching, with all the miles of rugged coast nearby.

She had to get to the Town Library quick, and find out all she could about Billy Bowlegs and what might be the location of his hidden treasure.

When you needed to find out something related to the hidden history of Cape Cod, even if you were a witch, the Town Library was the place to be.

The Lighthouse

Chapter Thirteen

The Girls Get Close

It was now mid-afternoon. Storm clouds were rolling in, and the girls were becoming exhausted.

Amy's pixie costume had started to droop, her iridescent wings flopping slowly behind her. They all looked worse for wear.

Fortunately, Veronica had come with several chocolate bars, which she had shared equally amongst all the girls. Each was able to have three small squares, which had kept them going so far.

Veronica had been about to throw a wrapper into the marsh grass when ElsBeth gently stopped her.

"Think of the creatures of the marsh."

Veronica looked confused.

ElsBeth explained. "The fish and birds will be attracted to the bright foil. They'll think it's a small silver fish and will try to eat it. But their insides will get torn up when they swallow it.

"We can't throw candy wrappers or plastic away in

nature. They can last practically forever. Any creatures who tangle with it or try to eat it will be hurt, or even killed. Never mind how ugly it is to see trash in the woods or marshes or on the dunes."

ElsBeth sadly shook her head.

Some of the girls looked at each other with guilty glances. ElsBeth's words struck home. They hadn't thought this through before.

They were thinking about the poor creatures when Amy, who had somehow gotten into the lead, froze. Carmen, close behind, didn't notice and ran into her. Veronica stumbled, just barely avoiding falling into Carmen.

The girls had nervously moved closer to each other and bunched together the nearer they got to the lighthouse. When Amy stopped quickly, the whole line of tired girls was jostled all around.

"Up there. I saw the lighthouse," Amy whispered and pointed ahead. "And I think I saw something move inside."

The girls looked up immediately. But the fog had thickened fast, and whatever was there had disappeared from sight.

"You, you … couldn't have seen anything," stuttered Carmen. "That lighthouse has been abandoned for fifty years."

"Maybe that's where the boys are," whispered Veronica.

No one took a step.

"No," ElsBeth was firm. "They are in Billy Bowlegs's cave. I just know it."

"How are we going to find the cave if no one knows where it is?" piped up Lisa Lee.

Lisa Lee was wearing an overlarge witch costume, caked with marsh mud all along the bottom. Her glasses kept slipping down her button nose, and she looked like an untidy, miniature witch professor.

Lisa Lee almost never said anything, so the girls paid attention when she spoke up with this sensible question.

Lisa Lee was always logical, even if she was way too quiet most of the time.

ElsBeth hadn't worked out how to find the pirate's cave yet. But she knew that if the boys had been seen on the road to the lighthouse, it must be nearby.

There was nothing else out this way. The lighthouse road went for five miles from town to the rocky point, and there were no side roads. There was only marshland, then open water.

The right cave had to be somewhere on the rocky point.

"Let's look for signs," she said. "Their bikes must be nearby. With Robert Hillman-Jones in charge, the boys would never walk very far."

They continued on.

As the girls were talking, they had closely approached, and then, not seeing it in the fog, they had passed by the old abandoned lighthouse.

Hearing the waves crash close on the rocks and feeling the salt spray, they stopped— just in time—and bumped into each other again.

They had come around to the ocean side. There was nowhere else to go.

"I can't see anything," Carmen whined.

The girls searched, but could see nothing. The fog was too heavy.

ElsBeth wasn't sure what to do. But having no other idea, she imagined a clear sky.

And, just as she had imagined it, the fog began to lift. There, behind them, the vague shape of the lighthouse appeared. And, at the base, a heap of bicycles had been hidden hastily, ditched any which way.

But more mysterious was a jet-black, fancy car with British license plates.

Veronica spoke up first. "I noticed that car around town in the last week or two. I don't know who it belongs to.

"What would tourists from England be doing out here in this weather?"

Carmen whispered, "Maybe it's not tourists. Maybe it's treasure hunters and they've got the boys and … " Carmen's lower lip began to quiver and tears filled her soft, dark eyes.

"Poor Nelson," cried Amy. "We never should have made fun of his ears."

"Pull yourself together, Amy," snapped Veronica.

ElsBeth tried to remain calm. After all, she was a witch. And no matter what the situation was, she knew she would have to deal with it.

"We can't panic. We're smarter than the boys, and even if they are captured we'll figure out a way to get them out … alive. We just have to find them first.

"Girls, from here on out we have to be quiet as field mice. We need to find out what the situation is, and come up with a plan. No crying or loud noises.

"We are going to find them. Now follow me."

ElsBeth led the girls to the rock outcrops. No one saw anything, though—except for rocks and more rocks.

Occasionally a spotted seal would swim by, his sleek head popping up, then he circled back.

Finally the seal's bark got through to ElsBeth.

In the tense search, she'd momentarily forgotten the most important thing. As a witch she had certain skills. She could communicate with all the creatures around, if she would only listen and pay attention.

The seal must have seen something, and she was certain he would help them find their classmates.

ElsBeth couldn't very well start barking like a seal in front of her friends. So to communicate with the sea creature, she sent a clear mental image of the boys in the seal's direction.

The seal barked back a little impatiently. "That's what I've been trying to tell you! They are in the cave, but bad men have them.

"You must be very careful. Better yet, go back and get help!"

He hastily added an introduction. "Sir Sam Seal, at your service, young witch."

This was much worse than she feared. She couldn't bring her friends into such danger.

She turned to them. "Veronica, can you take the others back to the lighthouse? I've got an idea now where the boys are. I'll find them and bring them back."

Veronica tried to argue. But ElsBeth had used a special

singing voice, to enchant, just a little. (Which really didn't count as a spell, she was sure.)

And one by one the girls turned and made their way back to the lighthouse.

Sam Seal said, "Well, witch, I guess you are determined to find them.

"But just remember. Many a soul has searched for Billy Bowlegs's treasure—and none who found it have ever returned to tell the tale."

ElsBeth gulped.

Then she boldly stuck her chin out. She barked back her answer in the seal's own language now that her classmates weren't around to hear. "Surely, none of them were witches."

"True enough, true enough," Sam called back. "Then follow me, little one."

Sir Sam swam slowly along close to the rocky shore while ElsBeth scrambled to keep up with him.

The seal became more and more solemn as he led ElsBeth closer and closer to what were certain earthly, and unearthly, dangers.

Finally they came to an opening half hidden by the rocks. But it was now partially underwater, as the tide had turned.

Sam Seal stopped, bobbed up and down, and nodded silently at the opening.

ElsBeth gulped again.

She felt in her pocket for her orange pumpkin flashlight. She lifted one foot, heavy with doubts and fears that now weighed on her, and forced a step toward the cave entrance—which was filling minute by minute with the rising tide.

Chapter Fourteen
Hannah Looks for Answers

Meanwhile, back at the small, dusty, jam-packed-full historical section of the town library, Hannah was making alarming discoveries of her own.

Beginning in the 1700's there were stories of the legendary pirate Billy Bowlegs and his band of cutthroats.

Apparently his one and only soft spot had been his love for his Cape Cod sweetheart Verity Hope.

The riches he had accumulated during his years of robbing the Spanish ships on the southern seas had never been located. The guess was that the treasure was left somewhere near his sweetheart's home in Harwich.

In several reports it was hinted there was a cave nearby that was crammed full of the gold and silver and jewels he'd captured. But his prize was noted to be cleverly and mysteriously hidden.

Since Hannah had moved from Salem all those years ago, she'd sometimes heard mention of the pirate and his treasure, but she never gave it much attention. She was a witch and had more important things to worry about—the crops, the weather, the fishermen's catch, the lives of the village people.

In the hundreds of years since the pirate's sudden disappearance many had looked, but no one had ever found so much as a single gold coin.

That is—no one had ever found the treasure and returned to tell about it.

According to the records, groups of men had gone in search of the pirate's booty five separate times, and each time had disappeared without a trace, never to be seen or heard from again.

She would have helped when these treasure hunters were lost, of course, but her hands were usually full preventing some other local disaster. She'd never gotten really involved in one of these searches ... until now.

Hannah kept looking for clues. There must be something here.

She decided to focus on the old maps in the library basement. There were many that tried to pinpoint Captain Billy's treasure, with X's marked all along the coast and several inland, as well. Some of the X's were even on the islands.

Hannah shook her head. There were too many possibilities. "Well, it doesn't appear the answer is here after all."

Just as she was closing the last faded chart, she heard a shout. She looked through the thick old panes of glass in the basement window and saw people running outside.

Sylvanas popped up on the granite sill a second later.

"ElsBeth and the rest of the second-grade girls are

missing, too," he hissed. "They must have gone in search of the boys."

Sylvanas normally held himself above the world's usual foolishness. He wasn't a cat who showed emotion. But this was ElsBeth.

"ElsBeth's a good enough witch to find them, but she's not experienced enough to get them out of any really serious trouble they've managed to get into.

"And my feral cat troops report trouble brewing. Trouble with a capital 'T.' "

Frustrated, Hannah said, "I've checked all the maps and there are just too many places they could be."

But Sylvanas had gathered other important information.

"Several wild cats saw the boys heading toward the old abandoned lighthouse around dawn.

"There's nothing else out that way. But none of these ignorant cats had the sense to follow them or got close enough to listen in—lazy creatures." He tried to hide his fear from Hannah beneath anger, but failed.

"ElsBeth and the girls were spotted several hours later headed in the same direction. They were taking the deer path through the marshes so they wouldn't be seen.

"Again, those brainless kittens didn't think to follow. And I'll have one of their nine lives from each of them for this!"

Sylvanas was spitting mad to be let down so by his fellow felines.

Just then, an exceptionally large osprey, circling above, cried loudly, and caught their attention.

"The girls are safe by the lighthouse. All but ElsBeth

have been spotted.

"There is a strange, black vehicle parked there, though. The windows are tinted, and even my sharp eyes can't see inside to check for the boys."

Hannah and Sylvanas wasted no time. Hannah stepped on her bicycle, muttered another speed-spell, and whirled down the cobblestone road with Sylvanas riding in the wicker basket—sphinxlike in his favorite pose and managing to look like an Egyptian cat king, despite the danger facing ElsBeth—and the bumps.

Meanwhile the Wampanoags, using their own methods, had come to the same conclusion. And at this very moment several small fishing boats were also closing in on the abandoned lighthouse.

Sir Sam Seal

Chapter Fifteen
In the Pirate Cave

Billy Bowlegs

ElsBeth had not turned on her flashlight yet.

She squeezed herself as close to one rock wall as she could and quietly slid forward. The entrance was long and narrow, and turned a corner in the distance.

A feeble light shone from just past the turn. She heard some muttered whispering and stopped. The voices sounded far too deep for Robert Hillman-Jones and the other second-grade boys.

She got her bearings and started slowly again toward the bend, careful not to splash the water beginning to pool on the cave floor.

As she moved in a little farther, she was surprised to realize that she could see rather well.

Then she heard Professor Badinoff, her familiar, squeaking out a greeting. He quickly added instructions.

"Don't use your eyes. You must rely on your hearing and sonar."

ElsBeth didn't know she even *had* sonar, but she tried sending out a little sound beam and found she could perceive when it hit the wall and bounced back to her. Echo perception.

In fact, when she thought she was "seeing," she had actually been using sonar without even thinking about it.

"Wow, thanks, Professor," she squeaked back to her friend.

"You can't use your flashlight," he said. "There are some bad men ahead and they've captured the boys.

"ElsBeth, be careful," he said in bat-speak.

As Professor Badinoff flew off ahead, a hand reached out of the dark and closed over her mouth.

ElsBeth's knees collapsed and she almost fainted.

Then Johnny Twofeathers's head popped up right in front of her face. Johnny was attached to the hand that covered her mouth.

ElsBeth slumped forward in relief and would have

spoken out loud, but Johnny pointed toward the bend in the cave and made the silence sign by drawing a finger over his lips.

He slowly released her.

ElsBeth took a deep breath. She was so happy to see her friend was OK.

Using sign language, Johnny told ElsBeth what had happened.

Johnny explained that Robert Hillman-Jones had overheard some strangers talking about pirate treasure. And he and the boys had followed the strangers for several weeks, every chance they could get. The boys had organized to take turns spying on the men after school and on the weekends.

Yesterday, the strangers let slip they had found something. Nelson had overheard them in the diner whispering about the old lighthouse. So Hillman-Jones decided they would all follow them today.

The boys made sure they were at the lighthouse this morning just after dawn, before the strangers would arrive. And they followed the men into the cave around noon.

Johnny Twofeathers was behind the others as lookout when something went wrong.

Nelson Hamm tripped over some loose rocks, and the men were alerted by the noise. They came back and the boys were rounded up and herded inside, except Johnny, who was far enough behind to slip back unnoticed.

Johnny had hidden outside the cave hoping to hear more and come up with a rescue plan. But had finally decided he had to go back in and get closer—just before ElsBeth came along.

"I'll go first," Johnny signed. Then added unnecessarily, "Be quiet."

ElsBeth hated to be told what to do, especially when it was what she was doing anyway. But she held her tongue and bravely followed.

It was up to her and Johnny to rescue their friends.

The two crept closer to the bend until they were able to peek around the corner, one at a time.

The cave went deep and long. It took a moment to take it all in.

The space seemed to be supported by huge, blackened beams and granite rocks, which had been placed to brace up the natural rock ceiling.

Johnny and ElsBeth could just make out a smaller, separate cavern that opened up in the shadows behind first large chamber.

Two men stood in the light of their lanterns at the far end of the main chamber.

They were big and held pistols. Both were dressed in brand new hiking clothes and had binoculars around their necks.

One of them had a Peterson Bird Guide book sticking out of his pocket.

ElsBeth wondered why bird watchers would be carrying guns and searching for pirate treasure. But she quickly figured out this was a simple disguise. They were trying to look like bird watching tourists.

Nearby, the second-grade boys huddled in a corner, wet and frightened.

One of the men spoke. "Well, what should we do with the little blighters?" He sounded a little like a pirate himself.

The other one looked something like Dr. Doolittle, and he spoke in a snobby sounding, British accent.

"Nothing," he said. "All the legends say no one's ever returned alive after looking for the treasure. We'll just make sure they are here at high tide and get washed to sea.

"Let's let Captain Bowlegs's curse and Father Neptune do our dirty work for us. It will be just another tragic accident," he added with a nasty little laugh.

The man straightened up and looked around. ElsBeth and Johnny ducked.

"It's hard to believe that what I heard from my great-grandfather turns out to be true." The man shook his head. "When the crazy old man told me tales of the family ancestor, Verity Hope, I didn't believe him. But then when I was cleaning out his chest, I found the map."

The man bent down. "Now, come and help me lift the trapdoor."

ElsBeth and Johnny Twofeathers watched fascinated as the two men hunched over to step into the smaller cave room. They grunted with the effort as they began to haul on a black iron ring attached to a heavy wooden trapdoor set firmly in the floor.

ElsBeth's mind whirled to find something to distract the men in the hope that the boys could escape.

A second later the men's persistent tugging suddenly paid off and the trapdoor came loose with a great sucking sound of mud letting go—a terribly rude sound, and

ElsBeth stifled the hysterical giggles that threatened to come out.

The one in the green and navy pullover grabbed his flashlight, looking like a mad underground cave explorer for a moment as the beam swung up and lit his face from below.

But when the light pointed into the space below, thousands of sparkles winked back.

From their higher position in the cave entrance ElsBeth and Johnny could both see there were broken chests of gold and glittering jewels.

The silver had turned black with age, so much so that amidst the bright, shiny treasure there were deep black holes that almost absorbed the light.

Though you couldn't tell in the cave, it was almost dusk now—a witching hour, in any case. And all the more powerful, as this was that most special night when the natural and spirit worlds merged—Halloween.

ElsBeth suddenly felt a shift, and she was no longer looking at a cave with age-blackened beams.

The wood was fresh and new, just like it was when originally put in place.

The men gleefully saw nothing but the treasure.

But they shifted nervously.

The one who sounded like a pirate lifted a blackened silver box to his face and began to lift its cover.

Then from behind him, a loud swoosh cut through the air.

And there was Billy Bowlegs, in the flesh, so to speak.

Well, not quite "flesh," but clearly it once was.

He held a long, curved sword, a cutlass, in his outstretched hand.

He wasn't tall, but he had about him a time-hardened meanness, and was completely scary, balanced on his wide bowlegs.

Then this real pirate boomed out to the treasure-hunting fake bird watchers, "Billy Bowlegs 'ere."

And with a deep laugh added, "Pleased to make yer acquaintance."

He leapt toward the men and smiled. "I always like to be polite 'afore I cut a man's 'ead off."

Feet frozen to floor, and with no appropriate response to a pirate ghost with a sword, one of the men screamed at the top of his lungs—sounding an awful lot like Carmen when she saw a mouse.

He dropped the silver box in his hands, and started swatting at what looked like two extremely angry humming birds buzzing around his head.

ElsBeth whispered, "Fairies! It is the two fairies Grandmother told me about!"

Having excellent hearing, the fairies flew right over to take a closer look at ElsBeth.

"Definitely a witch," said the one with the darker wings.

The other added, "Let's save it. It's cute."

ElsBeth didn't know what to think, or even how to think. But before she could, shots rang out toward the back of the cave.

The men were fighting fiercely with Billy Bowlegs for his precious treasure.

The boys in the corner huddled closer to each other, stiff with fear.

Johnny Twofeathers grabbed ElsBeth and pulled her toward the boys.

"Now's our chance. Come on. Let's get them out of here."

ElsBeth and Johnny, followed by the two fairies, and the huge bat, sped to the boys and pulled and pushed them to their feet.

Though nearly paralyzed with cold and terror, the boys started moving.

Robert Hillman-Jones looked up, as if he just awakened. "ElsBeth, you *can't* be here!" Then he fainted dead away.

Nelson and Frankie Sylvester grabbed his legs, and Johnny and ElsBeth took his arms, and they stumbled back toward the entrance.

Billy Bowlegs stopped mid-sword-sweep and yelled, "Arrrgh! They're escaping!" And took off after the young folk.

This made the prickly fairies angry, though, as they had decided on the spot to adopt ElsBeth and her friends.

They buzzed right up to the old pirate and started spinning around his head.

Their shiny wings beat so fast that all the pirate could see was a sparkling blur surrounding him.

"Blind me eyes!" he yelled, while poking at the fairies with his sword.

The two Englishmen took this opportunity to try to escape, grabbing as much loot as they could carry.

But before they got halfway across the cavern a slimy wall of frogs, boldly led by Bartholomew, bounded into view and hopped toward them.

All the men could do was slip and slide.

Then the fairies, tired of taunting the old pirate, also went after the treasure hunters.

With their tiny sharp teeth they nipped at the men's ears.

"Ow! Ouch!" the men screamed.

The classmates neared the entrance.

Nelson had dropped Hillman-Jones's legs a couple times, so Jimmy took over.

Nelson's strength began to fail further and he fell behind the others.

At the front now, Frankie Sylvester stopped and screamed, "Indians!"

He tried to dodge back into the cave.

Johnny Twofeathers and ElsBeth dropped Hillman-Jones altogether, and pushed ahead to the cave entrance.

It was quite a sight that greeted them.

There was a long canoe with two young Native Americans in what looked like war paint, but was really hunting camouflage they hadn't had time to wipe off when they'd been called to the search by Eddie Wily Coyote's alert.

They held antique harpoons (they'd grabbed from the Legion Hall, where they hung on the wall as decorations— just in case). And they had on florescent-orange hunting caps.

Hovering to the east was an ocean kayak manned by several strong Wampanoags, guided by a few members of Sir Sam Seal's family.

Several fishermen from the tribe in their waders, guarded the entrance to the cave, some kind of spiked fishing spears in their hands.

Behind them, offshore, was an old fishing trawler manned by several tribal elders wearing Red Sox baseball caps. A small dinghy with a ten horsepower outboard motor, captained by the Wampanoag medicine man Wily Coyote, headed toward shore.

In the bow of the dinghy, looking majestic while carefully keeping every single cat hair as far away from the water as possible, was Sylvanas, and right behind him was Hannah.

A thought crossed ElsBeth's mind that the intense cat now looked like a cross between a hedgehog and a puma, with all that black hair sticking straight up.

Johnny and ElsBeth smiled and waved their arms to attract attention, just as another shot rang out behind them.

Boys started popping out of the entrance and plopping into the water.

Frogs and toads were everywhere.

ElsBeth and Johnny grabbed Robert Hillman-Jones and shoved him onto a rock. Sir Sam took guard to keep him from slipping into the sea, juggling his head out of the water like a small bouncing ball.

Someone yelled, "Where's Nelson? He was right behind me."

ElsBeth and Johnny Twofeathers ran back toward the

cavern, now rapidly filling with the rising tide.

More shots rang out.

Professor Badinoff flew by ElsBeth's head and squeaked out, "Back there. Nelson's back there. He's down."

They moved deeper into the cavern.

Billy Bowlegs, looking wispier and less solid than before, continued fighting with the two Englishmen, who by now bled from several shallow cuts. Their ears were bright red with fairy bites.

The three battled around the open trap door, with the gold and glittering diamonds, rubies, emeralds and pearls lighting them from below.

With the force of the incoming tide, Nelson had been knocked off his feet and had floated back toward the fighting. He was breathing, but his arm was at a funny angle, and there was blood …

"We've got to save him," Johnny hollered. "ElsBeth, I know you're a witch. Do something … witchy."

ElsBeth was so stunned she dropped the pumpkin flashlight she'd been using to help light their way, and it clanged against a rock.

Both the pirate and the men heard this, and they focused on their new target.

There was no time to think. There was no time for permission. There was no time …

ElsBeth closed her eyes, became still, and let her voice

ring out, filling the cave with the most powerful spell she knew:

> *Birds of the air,*
> *Creatures of sea,*
> *Wind and water,*
> *Now come to ME!*

A huge wave rose up and crashed into the cavern, knocking over ElsBeth, Johnny and the two Englishmen.

Billy Bowlegs yelled out, "Shiver me timbers!" and he slashed again with his sword at the two men who thrashed in the water.

The wave pushed ElsBeth and Johnny farther into the cave and right beside Nelson.

"Grab his head!" Johnny yelled over the foamy surf.

ElsBeth and Johnny struggled but took up Nelson's dead weight. A great flock of birds and bats flew into the cave, and a ten-foot shark also swam silently past them.

"We need to get out now!" Johnny screamed.

An unnatural blast of wind then came up from the *back* of the cave, and the three youngsters were blown clear to the front entrance.

Screeching and screaming sounds rose behind them.

Out to sea, dark storm clouds brewed on the horizon. They all needed to get to safety fast. The boats wouldn't be able to stay out in this weather—the towering waves now crashing on the rocks foretold the fate of anyone who remained unsheltered near the sea.

But ElsBeth and Johnny no longer had the strength to hold onto Nelson. And Nelson had begun to say strange, dreamlike things.

They were so close. But maybe they wouldn't make it after all.

Neptune's powerful grip pulled down on their exhausted bodies. Down off the rocks to the sea.

Then strong hands from above pulled them even more powerfully up, and into the safety of the ocean kayak.

The last thing ElsBeth saw before she was pulled away was Grandmother and Sylvanas racing by in the dinghy. Tribal elder Eddie Wily Coyote's long braid whipped around him as he steered the craft at full speed through the waves, following close behind Sir Sam Seal who was now guiding them straight into the cave.

Chapter Sixteen

Back on Main Street

The Halloween celebrations had been cancelled, but everyone in town was so relieved all the young people were back safely that no one complained. Including the somewhat dazed girls who had been picked up at the lighthouse by the constable after the Wampanoag fishing trawler radioed in their position.

It was late but all the students gathered around Nelson's bed in Old Doc Mather's place on Quahog Drive.

Nelson had his arm set in a handsome, electric-blue cast, and was sitting up now, looking pale and weak, but smiling.

Amy, her fairy wings still drooping, sat in a small rocking chair by his side and held his hand.

Robert Hillman-Jones, in the next bed, was sitting up and boasting how they would go back and claim the treasure when Hannah and Sylvanas entered the room.

"What treasure?" she sang out in a musical voice, so enchanting that all around felt they must be dreaming.

"Pirates and golden treasure are legends surely."

It was very pleasant listening to Hannah, everyone felt relaxed.

"The boys got lost by the old lighthouse and found an old cave. They were trapped when the tide came in and the Wampanoags rescued them.

"Boys always look for treasure. But the pirate is just an old story, nothing more."

They all nodded their heads in agreement.

Robert Hillman-Jones tried to shake it off, but eventually started nodding, too.

Hannah then brightly announced, "It's Halloween!" And the spell was broken.

"The teachers have brought the party here!"

And there at the door was Ms. Finch dressed in shiny emerald green, looking like either a shimmering grasshopper or a large praying mantis. It wasn't really clear.

But she was smiling and carrying a lobster pot filled with candy.

Constable Sylvester muscled in a barrel for apple bobbing and began filling it with water.

Other teachers brought Halloween decorations and put them on the walls.

Outside the window, those that couldn't fit into Doc's place had started their own celebration.

It was, without a shade of doubt, turning into the best Halloween ever after all.

ElsBeth sat in the corner, hungrily eating chocolate,

which rapidly spread all over her face like some horrible skin disease.

Johnny Twofeathers sat next to her, also enjoying chocolate. The only difference was his chocolate was going into his mouth. Johnny had always been much neater than ElsBeth.

Worried it might change everything that Johnny now knew she was a witch, ElsBeth turned to him and said, "Chief, remember what you said to me back there in the cave?"

Johnny looked back at her blankly. "No. What did I say, ElsBeth?"

ElsBeth smiled, happy her grandmother had solved *that* problem with her enchantment, too. "Oh, nothing important."

Chapter Seventeen
The Pirate's Future

Home

Back at home that night ElsBeth got up her nerve and said, "Grandmother, I have a confession to make."

Grandmother was tucking ElsBeth into her snug captain's bed with her puffy, blue, half-moon comforter.

"What is it, dear?"

"Well, er … well, er … you know I was never, ever, ever, under any circumstances, to use witchery unless you were directly supervising me."

"Yes, ElsBeth." Her grandmother looked serious.

"Er … today in the cave, er … I did it," ElsBeth stammered.

"Well, dear, you'll find out that there are rare times when the right thing to do is to do what you know is right, even if it breaks a rule.

"But I was nearby, and you did just fine."

Hannah beamed down on the little witch.

ElsBeth smiled back, half asleep now.

"Grandmother, what will happen to Billy Bowlegs and his treasure?"

Her grandmother said, "Well, the boys have already forgotten.

"The cave is underwater again, and will be for another fifty years before the tides are just right to allow entrance.

"I imagine the deal Wily Coyote and I struck with Billy Bowlegs at the cave will stand. He gets to keep his treasure secret and all to himself for the next fifty years. And then when the moon is full, and it's Halloween, and the tides are just right, maybe a treasure hunter will come along and dare to match wits and courage with the famous pirate again.

"He quite enjoys it, you know."

ElsBeth was drifting off. She was thinking of pirates and gold, of frogs and bats, and talking seals.

She smiled. Life was certainly grand and full of adventure.

And with that true thought, ElsBeth fell sleep.

THE END

ElsBeth's Further Adventures

All are again hopeful in the small Cape village, and life goes on. But what sort of adventure … or trouble … will the young witch and her friends find themselves involved in next in the *Cape Cod Witch Series?*

Book II, *ElsBeth and the Freedom Fighters*—Follow ElsBeth and her friends on a field trip to Boston's Freedom Trail, and then across treacherous waters to Nantucket Island in their daring attempt to rescue a kidnapped Arabian prince.

Fast-paced, adventurous and fun, Book II includes a treasure chest of historical nuggets and Cape and Islands lore, and is loosely based on the story of a real-life freedom fighter privateer from the revolutionary period of this country.

Book III, *ElsBeth and the Call of the Castle Ghosties*— When their ancestral home and lands are threatened in a way not ever before seen in their far-reaching pasts, three ancient ghosts need one of their clan from the living world. They call the young Cape Cod witch across the sea to the old country.

Not yet proven or highly skilled, but with a personal calling to protect the natural world, and her own need to find out more about the family mysteries, ElsBeth is in well above her magic level.

The award winning *The Little Cape Cod Witch Cookbook, The Secret Recipes of Hannah Goodspell*—Wholesome, tasty treats you can make with a grown-up helper and enjoy with friends. The cookbook includes full-color illustrations, stories and fun cooking facts. Find out how "Cooking is a kind of magic!"

Visit *www.CapeCodWitch.com*
to find out more!

Dedication

This book is dedicated to the magic of Cape Cod and the Islands,

And to Emelia, the littlest Bean—
May your life always be an adventure!

Acknowledgement

I would like to extend a special thank you to Bill Hiss of Bates College for his kind editorial assistance. Any remaining errors are the sole responsibility of the author.

Author and Illustrator

Author J Bean Palmer

In the *Cape Cod Witch Series,* J Bean calls upon her family's long history in New England including a Revolutionary "Green Mountain Boy," Cape Cod cranberry farmers and artists, and an oft-told family legend that as her grandmother's ancestors stepped off the *Mayflower*, her grandfather's relatives were there to greet them. With a degree in Environmental Science, the author's ElsBeth stories reflect a passion and respect for the natural world and its magical kinship.

Illustrator Melanie Therrien

Illustrator Melanie Therrien lives in western Maine with her husband Glenn, their dog Tito, and three cats, one of which was the model for Sylvanas in the ElsBeth books. The juried fine artist looks to the state's natural beauty for inspiration for her fanciful images and landscapes. The stylistic artwork for the *Cape Cod Witch Series* is her first book illustration project. The artist may be contacted at *www.wickedillustrations.com.*

CPSIA information can be obtained
at www.ICGtesting.com
Printed in the USA
BVHW092123220819
556531BV00003B/78/P